Illustrated by Jan Smith

Customer Service: 1-800-595-8484 or customer_service@pilbooks.com

www.pilbooks.com

p i kids is a registered trademark of Publications International, Ltd.
Look and Find is a registered trademark of Publications International, Ltd.,
in the United States and in Canada.

8 7 6 5 4 3 2 1

ISBN-13: 978-1-4508-2115-5
ISBN-10: 1-4508-2115-4

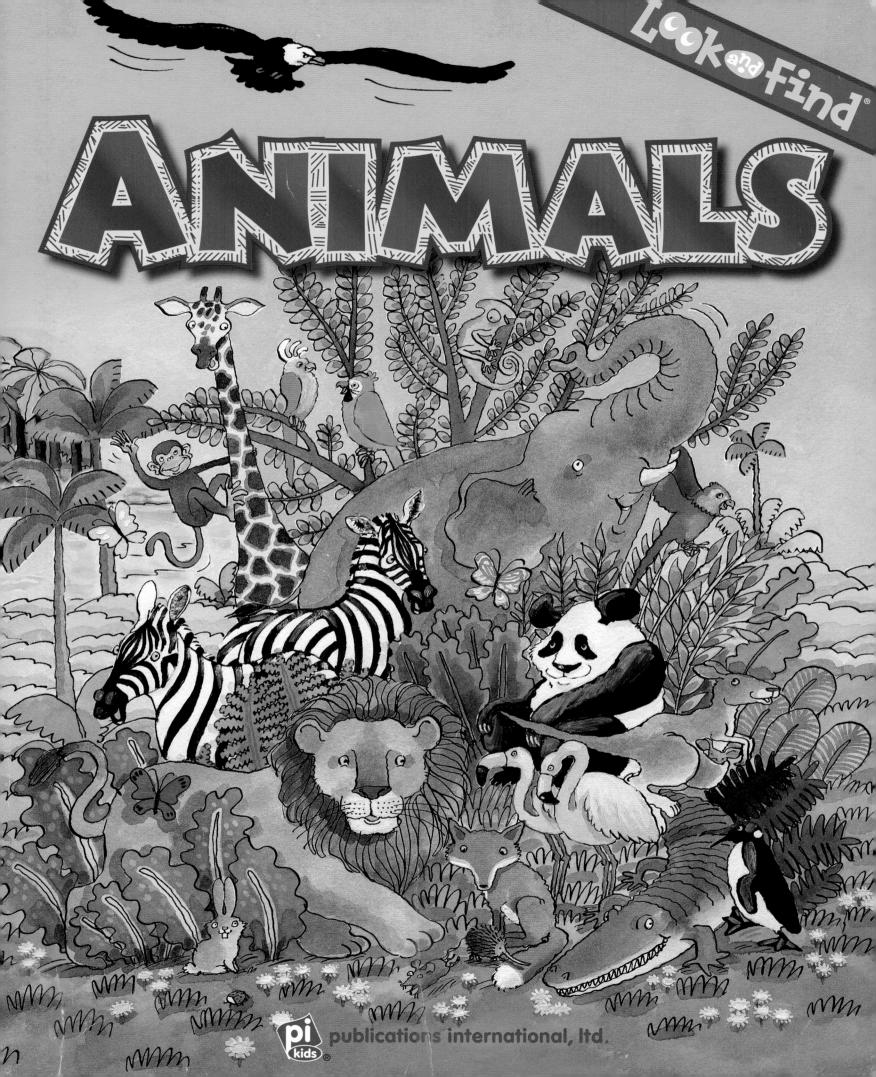

ANIMALS

Look and Find®

pi kids®

publications international, ltd.

Be careful! This jungle is simply crawling with man-eating cats and aggressive primates. *Shh!* Did you hear that? As you make your way through, try to spot these jungle animals.

Sloth

Toucan

Tiger

Anteater

Parrot

Jaguar

Find higher ground! That's not an earthquake you feel—it's a stampede of wildebeests! Can you make out these wildebeests in the chaos?

Dive for cover! Those hammerhead sharks and that great white are about to duke it out on the great coral reef! As you hide, keep an eye out for these ocean animals.

Clownfish

Crab

Anemone

Puffer fish

Starfish

Angelfish

Whatever you do, keep your hands in the boat! There's a granddaddy gator around here that'll have you for lunch if you don't. Can you spot him and these other swamp animals?

River otter

Heron

Turtle

Beaver

Frog

Alligator

That isn't a flock of bird flying overhead! At dusk, hundreds of bats leave their cave to find food. Can you find these other nocturnal creatures?

Raccoon

Cricket

Owl

Opossum

Cat

Badger

The forest animals are nervous because there's a bear nearby! Could be hungry...and ferocious. Find the bear and these other forest animals.

Fox

Moose

Skunk

Deer

Gray wolf cub

Bear

Brr! It's hard, but you have to keep moving—even in this extreme cold. You never know when a hungry polar bear is going to catch your scent. It's especially dangerous to see a cub nearby. Can you find the cub and these other cold-weather animals?

Wolverine

Polar bear cub

Walrus

Puffin

Caribou

Musk ox

Go back and find these monkeys in the jungle.

Go back to the savanna and find these animals.

Ostrich

Lion

Rhino

Cheetah

Gazelle

Zebra

Go back to the ocean and find these sea turtles.

Go back to the swamp and find these bugs.

Dragonfly

Butterfly

Ladybug

Beetle

Snail

Spider

Go back to the bats' cave and find 10 fireflies.

Go back to the forest and find these animals and insects.

Butterfly

Woodpecker

Opossum

Mouse

Chipmunk

Bee

Go back to the desert and find these lizards.

Go back and find these animals that are nearly blending into the snow.

Ermine

Arctic fox

Arctic hare

Snowy owl

Arctic wolf

Harp seal